D1357867

ELLiE
ULTRA

Ellie Ultra is published by Stone Arch Books,
A Capstone Imprint
1710 Roe Crest Drive
North Mankato, Minnesota 56003
www.mycapstone.com

Library of Congress Cataloging-in-Publication Data is available on the Library of Congress website.

ISBN: 978-1-4965-3139-1 (hardcover) — 978-1-4965-3144-5 (paperback) — 978-1-4965-3148-3 (ebook PDF) — 978-1-4965-3152-0 (reflowable epub)

Summary: Ellie can't wait for her first day at Winkopolis Elementary School. But she soon learns that her superpowers make her stand out in a not-so-super way.

Editor: Alison Deering
Designer: Hilary Wacholz

Printed in the United States of America.
009662F16

An *Extra*-Ordinary Girl

written by Gina Bellisario

illustrated by Jessika von Innerebner

STONE ARCH BOOKS
a capstone imprint

TABLE OF CONTENTS

CHAPTER 1

Extraordinary Ellie

It was just another day in the city of Winkopolis. Doggies napped. Babies drooled. Neighbors chatted. Everyone was busy doing the same old ordinary things. Everyone except for the girl who lived at 8 Louise Lane.

That girl was Ellie Ultra. She was getting ready for school, quicker than a cheetah in a turbocharged rocket. It was *extra*ordinary.

In a blink, Ellie bolted out of bed. "Oops!" she said, skidding to a stop. Her hot heels left burn marks on the rug. "I almost forgot!"

Ellie circled back around, fast as lightning. *Flump!* went her blanket. *Plunk!* went her pillow. She made her bed in two seconds flat. That way her parents wouldn't remind her — again. Then she turned to X-ray her room.

"Super Fluffy!" Ellie cheered, spotting her stuffed dog behind the bookshelf. "I thought a super-villain had gotten you." She plucked him out of his hiding spot, gave him a quick cuddle, and then left him on her bed.

At her closet, beams shot out of Ellie's eyes like mini-flashlights. She X-rayed the doors, revealing her clothes behind them. The beams scanned left to right and top to bottom. Finally, they stopped and flickered — perfect outfit located!

Reaching inside, Ellie took out her Princess Power shirt and some striped leggings. In a blur, she was dressed.

After sweeping a headband into her dark curls to hold her hair out of her face, Ellie shot into the air and rocketed downstairs.

In the kitchen, Dad had just plunked down a bowl of blueberries-and-cream oatmeal. “Here’s your super-delicious breakfast,” he said as Ellie swooped into her seat. “Eat up, third grader.”

“Are you ready to start school?” Mom asked, taking milk out of the fridge.

“Yes!” Ellie answered. “I’ve been waiting for three years, one month, nine days, and six seconds . . .” She paused, checking her watch. “Seven seconds, actually.”

She had been counting the minutes until she could attend Winkopolis Elementary School for as long as she could remember. But first, she’d had some important things to learn at home, with her parents as her teachers.

In kindergarten, they'd taught her death-ray safety. In first grade, she'd learned how to stump an evil mastermind. And in second grade? That year they'd quizzed her on every super-villain in Winkopolis. Naming their weaknesses had counted for extra credit.

It hadn't been ordinary school, but Ellie's parents weren't exactly ordinary. They were super-genius scientists who worked for a special group called B.R.A.I.N. Ellie wasn't sure what *B.R.A.I.N.* stood for — only the actual members knew that — but she knew the group squashed super-villains, just like she did. After all, Ellie was a superhero!

But even superheroes needed to eat breakfast. Ellie tried a scoop of oatmeal. It had cooled off, so she heated it up. Cupping the bowl, her hands glowed red-hot and warmed the oatmeal all the way through.

"Two hundred and twelve degrees," Ellie said as steam swirled in berry-sweet loop-de-loops. "Perfect!"

Mom handed her the milk, and in one gulp, Ellie emptied the carton. Then she let out a deafening *BURP!* that sent rumblings through the house.

Dad scrunched his forehead. "It sounds like somebody needs a super helping of manners," he said, catching a bite of egg before Ellie's burp could send it jiggling off his plate.

Ellie smiled weakly. "Excuse me."

"You're going to love Winkopolis Elementary School," Mom said. "You'll be able to meet lots of new friends. And the school year just started last week, so you won't have missed much."

Friends! Ellie thought. All her super life, she had been busy thwarting evildoers and rescuing the good citizens of Winkopolis. She never had time to play with other kids — this was her chance!

Ellie wiped her milk mustache. "The kids are probably still talking about what they did during summer break. Maybe I can tell everyone how I foiled the Winkopolis Bank robbery! Or maybe how Dad turned my room into my own secret hideout? Or . . . I know! Maybe I can talk about how I stopped that meteor from crashing into the moon? That was fun!"

"Why don't you talk about our trip to the zoo?" Mom suggested.

"That time I saved the baby hippo?" Ellie said, her eyes brightening with excitement. Everyone in town already knew about Ellie's superpowers. But she was sure the other kids would be extra impressed when they heard about all she'd done.

Her mom winked. "That's exactly what I was thinking."

"Better get a move on," Dad said, glancing at the clock. "You don't want to be late for your first day."

Ellie quickly finished her oatmeal. She also ate two-dozen eggs, a stack of pancakes, and enough bananas to feed a family of gorillas. It was an out-of-the-ordinary breakfast, but it was just right for Ellie. After all, she was an *extra*ordinary girl.

"One more thing," Mom said before Ellie left the table. She pulled out a shiny pink cloth. "Ta-da!"

"A cape!" Ellie squealed. She'd been begging her parents for one for months! Every honest-to-goodness superhero had a cape. And given that she was an honest-to-goodness superhero, Ellie *had* to have one.

Ellie fastened the cape around her shoulders and grabbed her backpack. "Now all I need is a superhero name."

"Hmm . . . how about Super Student?" Dad replied. "But that will only work if you have the power of being punctual. Off you go!"

CHAPTER 2

BLAM!

Moments later, all the way across town, kids shuffled through the main doors of Winkopolis Elementary School. "Good morning, students!" a tall man wearing a suit and a friendly smile greeted them.

Ellie scooted along with the crowd. She had already arrived, thanks to her lightning-fast flight. Her cape had helped her soar on the wind like a jet's wings.

Curious to find out who the man was, she read his mind:

Name: *Mr. Cleveland, principal*

Favorite Things: *corned beef sandwiches, Winkopolis Sluggers baseball team, school assemblies, summer vacation*

Not-So-Favorite Things: *flu season, bullies, end-of-summer vacation*

"You must be Ellie Ultra, our new student," Mr. Cleveland said as Ellie walked up. "I'm Mr. Cleveland, the school principal. I'll show you to your classroom."

How did he know my name? Ellie thought, following him inside. If Mr. Cleveland had read her mind, maybe he was a superhero too!

They walked past the auditorium and the main office. Outside the library, Ellie spotted a cardboard cutout of her all-time favorite comic book superhero — Princess Power. Attached to the cutout, a speech bubble said: *Reading gives you POWER!*

"Princess Power!" Ellie exclaimed.

"Are you a comic book fan?" Mr. Cleveland asked.

Ellie nodded quickly. "I like Maximum Mouse, Mind Surfer, and the Zombie-Eating Pumpkin, but I *love* Princess Power. She fights the Troll King and protects Sparkle Kingdom." She thought for a second. "I would fight a troll if one ever came to Winkopolis."

Mr. Cleveland raised an eyebrow. "Let's hope you never have to," he said.

Ellie smiled to be nice. But after fighting a mutant hot dog the week before, she knew anything was possible.

Mr. Cleveland came to a stop in front of Room #128. "Here we are."

A woman was waiting at the door. She had pink cheeks and kind eyes, and she smelled like a lily. A calla lily, according to Ellie's super sniffer.

"Hi, Ellie," the woman said. "I've been expecting you. Welcome to our classroom. My name is Miss Little, and I'm your teacher."

Mr. Cleveland excused himself, and Miss Little showed Ellie to her locker in the hallway. "Would you like to put away your, um, cape?" she asked.

"No, thank you," Ellie replied politely. "It helps me fly, especially at high altitudes."

Miss Little frowned ever so slightly. "I see."

As they entered the classroom, Ellie stopped fast. Her pencils rolled out of her arms. All around her, kids played computer games. Some read on the story rug, which was shaped like the United States of America, while others doodled at their desks.

Ellie was confused. *Why isn't anybody playing laser leapfrog? Why isn't anybody swimming with electric eels?* The kids weren't doing any of the activities she did at home in super school.

"Okay, everybody!" Miss Little announced. "Please take your seats. It's Share Time."

Ellie scanned the room for an empty desk. There was one by the window, next to a boy with spiky red hair. He was scribbling something in his notebook. Maybe he would be her first friend!

Ellie skipped over and peeked at what he was writing. Her eyes narrowed at the page. It read:

My Plan for World Domination
by Dex Diggs, evil mastermind

STOP ALL SUPERHEROES!

As soon as he caught her looking, Dex clapped his notebook closed. "Hey, no peeking!" he said, his face

IMAGINATION IS MORE IMPORTANT THAN KNOWLEDGE.
-EINSTEIN

souring. With his hair sticking up, he looked like a rotten pineapple.

Ellie gulped as she sat down. *First friend? More like first archenemy.*

Miss Little took her spot at the front of the class. “Before Share Time, I want to introduce our new student, Ellie Ultra,” she said. “Welcome aboard, Ellie. Now, who would like to share something special with the class?”

A boy in the next row raised his hand. Ellie saw that his name tag read *Joshua*. “I had a soccer tournament yesterday,” he said. “I scored two goals!”

“I had a gymnastics meet,” a girl whose name tag read *Amanda* volunteered. She held up a silver medal for everyone to see. “I came in second.”

As more and more kids raised their hands, Ellie grew more and more excited. She couldn’t wait to join in. She thought and thought about what she could say. Finally, her hand shot up.

"Yes, Ellie?" Miss Little said.

"On Saturday, I got to stay up late," Ellie replied proudly. "I had to stop an army of radioactive ants."

Whispers rose up around the room, and Amanda squirmed a little in her seat. "Radioactive ants? Weird!"

As the whole class stared and whispered, Dex pointed at Ellie. "There's a radioactive ant on your shirt!"

Ellie looked down but only saw the Princess Power logo. He'd tricked her!

"That's enough, Dex," Miss Little said. She put a stop-sign sticker on his behavior chart.

Dex's lip curled into a frown at the sight of the sticker. Then he made another rotten-pineapple face at Ellie. This time, it was rottener.

Ellie's spirits sank like a robot shark without batteries. Sharing her super activity hadn't gone as well as she'd thought. In fact, the other kids seemed to think it was super weird.

* * *

As the day went on, things didn't get any better.

At recess, Amanda tried to tag Ellie, but Ellie's super speed made catching her impossible. "I give up," Amanda said, doubled-over.

In math, when the class worked on estimating, Ellie was the only one who rounded her answer to the nearest quadrillion.

"To the nearest ten, please," Miss Little kindly reminded her.

Before gym, everybody gathered around to guess what was inside the Mystery Box. Miss Little read the clues: "I'm a citrus fruit and round like a basketball. I'm also packed with vitamin C. What am I?"

It's an orange! Ellie thought. To check if she was right, she X-rayed the box.

"Awww!" Owen whined as Ellie's eye beams revealed the orange inside. "I was totally going to guess that."

While the class lined up for gym, Ellie tried to apologize, but Owen pretended not to hear. Ellie felt awful.

The gym teacher, Mrs. Walker, blew her whistle. "It's time for a soccer game!" she exclaimed. "The yellow team is playing the orange team. Grab a colored wristband, and take the field."

Score! Ellie thought as everyone crowded around the supplies tray to get wristbands. *If I get a point for my team, everyone will definitely like me. Owen might even forget about the Mystery Box!*

Of course, using a super-villain's memory-eraser on him would make him completely forget. But operating anything related to super-villains was a big no-no for superheroes. Ellie knew that. So instead, she took a yellow wristband and raced into position.

The game got off to a speedy start. Payton's soccer-star footwork helped the orange team take the lead, two to zero.

As Ellie waited near the goal, Hannah passed the ball to her. "Score, Ellie! We can still catch up!" she cheered.

Now is my chance! Ellie thought. With a super *oomph!* she gave the ball a strong kick.

BLAM! It rocketed through the net and disappeared down the field.

"Whoa," Owen said quietly. He was the goalie, but thankfully the ball had missed him. He'd been too busy crawling through the grass, hunting for a four-leaf clover, to try to block Ellie's shot. Lucky him!

Mrs. Walker peered through the hole in the net. "It looks like the game is over for today," she said. "The final score is two to one, which means the orange team has won. But good effort, everybody!"

The yellow team groaned as the orange team cheered and high-fived. Ellie stared down at the ground, too sad to say anything. Her team had lost the game, and it was all her fault.

"Is your superhero name Super Blooper?" Dex teased Ellie. "Or what about Goof Girl?" His words stung like a swarm of venomous wasps. If making her feel not so super was part of his evil plan, it was working.

CHAPTER 3

Power Off

After school, Ellie walked home. She didn't feel up to flying. She had tried super hard to make friends, but everything had been a bust. A bust with a capital *B-L-A-M!* The other kids thought she didn't belong. She knew it, even without reading their minds.

Ellie dragged her backpack up the walkway lined with purple-and-white gladiolas and trudged inside. She dropped her cape on the coat hook with a sigh.

“Mom? Dad?” Ellie called, wishing they were at home. She felt lonely, and even though her folks could act a little strange, they made good company.

Nobody answered.

They’re probably working — saving the world, Ellie thought.

To help B.R.A.I.N. fight the universe’s toughest villains, Mr. and Mrs. Ultra invented extraordinary gadgets. They’d built the Ultra Monster Maker, which could scare the scales off the snakiest bad guy. They’d also created useful gadgets like the Ultra Flavor Booster, which could make broccoli taste like a chocolate cake.

Her parents weren’t normal, but nobody seemed to care. Maybe they would know how she could fit in? After all, just last week, they’d figured out how to take the stink out of a stinkbug. Compared to that, solving Ellie’s problem would be easy — and less smelly.

Ellie floated downstairs to their underground laboratory. "Hellooo?" she called out, popping her head in the doorway.

She saw her parents behind the glass walls of the testing station. Ellie's eyes twinkled. Testing a gadget was always her parents' final step before finishing it. What were they cooking up for B.R.A.I.N. this time?

Ellie made her way past bubbling beakers and dripping doodads. "Hi, Cyclops," she said to the lab's giant, one-eyed iguana. He waved from inside his tank, and then went back to finger-painting.

Mrs. Ultra noticed Ellie and jumped up from her desk. She was wearing her Ultra Safety Suit, which made Ellie giggle. The suit helped keep her parents safe while they tested a new gadget, but it also made them look like life-size marshmallows.

"Come see our new invention!" Mom called. When Ellie stepped inside the station, Mrs. Ultra held out

a small remote. It was short and thin with a square button in the center. "It's called the Ultra Remote," Mom explained. "One click lets you control *anything*. You could make a rooster sound like a donkey or turn the mayor into a tight-rope walker or . . ."

Mom's voice trailed off as Ellie's supersonic hearing picked up a noise outside. It sounded like a whirring fan.

"Uh-oh," Dad said, eyeing the Ultra I-Spy Cam, "looks like we have guests."

Ellie peeked over his shoulder. Sure enough, a spaceship of evil alien blobs was onscreen. It hovered one mile above the Ultras' house and then began dropping closer and closer, probably coming to steal some gadget. Since Mr. and Mrs. Ultra made super-powerful stuff, villainous visitors were always trying to take something.

Mrs. Ultra pointed the Ultra Remote at the camera. "Away," she said, clicking the button.

Onscreen, the spaceship shot away like an airborne rubber band.

Mom shook her head. "I'd know those slime buckets anywhere. That was Captain Blob and the Goo Crew."

Ellie had never gone up against Captain Blob and the Goo Crew, but she remembered seeing them on B.R.A.I.N.'s Most Wanted Super-Villains List. They were the biggest troublemakers in the galaxy.

"They must've spotted the Ultra Remote," Mom said. "They've been on the lookout for a way to control the universe, and they probably think this will do the trick. Let's hope that warning shot keeps them away for good." She placed the remote on her desk and turned to Ellie. "So, how did your first day go?"

Ellie shrugged. "My teacher's nice, and the classes are okay. But I'm not sure I fit in with the other kids. I want them to like me, but I don't know how to make that happen."

Mom gave her a big, marshmallowy hug. "Let them get to know you. I'm sure they'll like you once they see how super you are."

"Maybe you're right," Ellie said. But privately she wondered if things might be easier if she was *un*-super.

* * *

"Want to play Guess That Super-Villain?" Mom asked Ellie after dinner.

Ellie shook her head no. Usually, she went wild for that game, but today she needed to focus on solving her school troubles. She headed to her room and curled up with a stack of comic books. "These might give me an idea," she said to herself.

Sure enough, sometime between *Mind Surfer vs. The Brain Wave* and *Maximum Mouse #12: Kitty Litter Strikes Cheesetown,* a thought struck her like a *POW*er-packed punch — to belong, the superheroes hid their super selves.

"When the superheroes aren't saving anybody they're . . . ordinary," Ellie said. "Ice Boy is a regular boy. Mind Surfer is a regular surfer. Even the Zombie-Eating Pumpkin is a regular pumpkin before midnight."

Ellie flipped through her favorite comic, *Princess Power, Protector of Sparkle Kingdom*. After defeating the Troll King, Princess Power turned back into a regular princess.

Deep in thought, Ellie squeezed her eyebrows together. How could she turn off her powers? She couldn't exactly give them a time-out. Suddenly it hit her. *But I* can *control my powers. All I need is the Ultra Remote!*

Racing down to the lab, Ellie blinked herself invisible and slipped past her parents. Then she took the Ultra Remote from her mom's desk. She bit her lip as she studied the tiny box. She felt a little bad taking it. After all, the remote belonged to her parents, not Ellie. But still, their work was for the greater good.

And if the Ultra Remote can help me make friends, it'll be better than good, Ellie thought. *It'll be great!*

CHAPTER 4

A Little Control

As soon as Ellie finished breakfast the next morning, she flew over to the door and grabbed her backpack. “In you go, super-genius invention,” she said as she dropped the Ultra Remote inside. “I hope you know how to control a superhero.”

Dad came around the corner. “Aren’t you forgetting something?” he asked.

Ellie’s eyes grew as big as Captain Blob and the Goo Crew’s flying saucer. Dad knew she had the remote!

But Dad simply reached over and took Ellie's cape off the hook. He held it out to her, and Ellie breathed a sigh of relief. So *that* was what he was talking about.

Ellie waved the cape away. "I'm not wearing that today." She hoped Dad wouldn't ask anything else. He was a genius, and geniuses always asked questions. It was how they got so smart.

Dad raised a curious eyebrow, but all he said was, "Oh, okay. Have a super day!"

Ellie smiled and nodded. But if everything went according to plan, today would be totally *un*-super.

* * *

When she got to school, Ellie headed straight for her locker. There, she unzipped her backpack, dug through her Cupcake Friends pencil toppers, and grabbed the Ultra Remote.

"Watch this!" a voice exclaimed.

Ellie whirled around and saw Hannah, Amanda, and Payton, three girls from her class, across the hall. Hannah was showing them some ballet moves. As Ellie had learned yesterday during Share Time, Hannah loved to dance. She had taken jazz and tap classes, and now she was in ballet.

"This is called a *pirouette,*" Hannah said. She twirled on her tippy toes like a ballerina puppet on strings.

"Wow! That was so good!" Amanda and Payton cheered. They took turns trying to copy Hannah.

Ellie walked over to the girls. "Can I try?" she asked. She had taken ballet in the spring. During the class recital, she'd twirled fast enough to turn into a tornado. That had been the end of ballet. But now that she had the Ultra Remote, Ellie could control her super speed.

"Sure," Hannah replied.

As the girls made room, Ellie turned away. "Spin," she said under her breath, clicking the Ultra Remote.

Ellie's body jerked obediently, and she rotated in one neat, perfect circle. The *pirouette* was pretty plain, but Elle thought it was plainly perfect.

"You're a great dancer!" Hannah said as Amanda and Payton clapped. "I have some pictures from my tap recital. They're in my desk. Want to see them?"

"Yes!" Ellie answered brightly. By clicking away her superpower, she suddenly belonged. It was as if she had blended in with the girls, without even turning invisible. The Ultra Remote was a success!

Ellie followed her new friends to their classroom, where she looked at Hannah's pictures with Amanda and Payton. After promising to play with them at recess, it was time for math.

Miss Little opened her teacher's workbook and read an estimation problem out loud. "Joey's mom makes twenty-five fish sticks. Joey and his teammates eat twelve after football practice.

Rounded to the nearest ten, how many fish sticks are left?"

Everybody started to figure out the answer, except for Ellie. Her super brain wasn't cooperating. By the time Miss Little finished speaking, it had already taken the number of fish sticks, divided them between Joey and his teammates, and multiplied the order in case Joey's coaches were hungry too.

Ellie sighed. Sometimes her mind was harder to control than a mechanical bull. Before it could add orders for tartar sauce, she clicked the remote under her desk. "Solve," she whispered.

In a blink, Ellie's mind went blank. In the next blink, one number appeared. Her hand flew up into the air.

"Ellie?" Miss Little asked, rubbing her chin nervously. She'd never had a student who rounded to the nearest quadrillion before.

"Ten," Ellie said calmly.

Miss Little's chin fell into her hand. "Bravo! That's right," she said. "It sounds like you'd make a helpful estimating partner. Maybe you can pair up with Dex? I'm sure he'd appreciate the help."

Ellie snuck a peek at Dex. He was glaring menacingly at Miss Little, probably plotting how to escape her plan. Obviously, Miss Little didn't know he was a super-villain. A super-villain would never accept a superhero's help, not in a rounded-to-the-nearest-quadrillion years!

* * *

Over the next few days, school was superly un-super. At recess, Ellie played tag with Hannah, Amanda, and Payton. She had no trouble controlling her super speed and even got tagged. When Miss Little brought out the Mystery Box, Ellie clicked off her X-ray vision. That way she wouldn't accidentally spoil the surprise. It was fun guessing at the clues, but it was Owen who guessed correctly — there was a cactus inside!

Before gym on Friday, Ellie tucked the Ultra Remote into her pocket. The soccer net had been fixed, but still. One hole in the goal had been enough.

Mrs. Walker had said that Ellie was the first kid in the history of Winkopolis Elementary School to score like that. It should've made Ellie feel awesome. But she still felt super blooperish.

"Listen up, class!" Mrs. Walker said. "Take your wristbands and positions. It's time to play a super game of soccer!"

She means an un-*super game,* Ellie thought, grabbing a yellow wristband from the supplies tray.

"Does anybody else want to be the goalie?" Owen asked at the orange team's net. Clearly, he was worried about another ball rocketing toward him. His teammates must have felt the same, because no one offered.

With a sigh, Owen got into position, and Mrs. Walker blew her whistle to start the game. It was an exciting match. Payton scored a goal for the orange team, then stole the ball away from Dex and scored again. After Joshua blocked Payton's third try, Amanda got a goal for the yellow team. Then Dex tied up the score, making it two to two.

"One minute left!" Mrs. Walker called out.

Ellie waited by the orange team's goal, hoping someone would pass her the ball. Then she could click the remote and kick a win for her team!

As if it had read her mind, the ball came rolling toward her.

"Ellie, you're open!" Hannah called. "Score!"

"Score! Score!" her teammates echoed.

Ellie's thumb pressed firmly on the Ultra Remote's button. "Kick," she whispered, and her leg swung back automatically. With a smooth and steady bump, the ball rolled forward.

Owen dove out of the way as the ball bounced squarely into the net. Goal! Mrs. Walker's whistle blew. Ellie and her teammates had won! Hannah ran up and gave Ellie a big hug.

"Super Blooper to the rescue!" Dex shouted.

Ellie ignored him. She was too busy smiling. The Ultra Remote was starting to make her feel ordinary — even if she didn't feel completely like herself.

CHAPTER 5

Smarty-Pants Parents

Over the weekend, Ellie got an unexpected call from Hannah.

"I got my costume for my ballet recital!" Hannah squealed through the phone. "You have to come see it. It's *so* cool."

Ellie beamed. Hannah was inviting her over! She raced into the laundry room, where her parents were fixing the Ultra Washing Machine. It had gotten jammed during the wash-rinse-dry-fold cycle. “Can I go to Hannah’s house?” she asked.

Mom looked up from her toolbox. “Sure. Be back in an hour, okay?”

Just then, Dad jumped out from behind the machine. “EUREKA! I found what was stuck in the motor.” He held up a pair of his underwear, which was covered in pictures of miniature microscopes.

Ellie crinkled her forehead. No doubt about it, she had the strangest super-genius scientist parents ever.

* * *

Whoosh! Ellie flew out the front door. Houses blurred as she streaked down the street. Seconds after she’d hung up the phone, Ellie rang Hannah’s doorbell.

Hannah greeted her with a big grin. "Wow! You got here fast," she said.

Ellie smiled weakly as she walked inside. Flying made getting anywhere easier, but she didn't tell her friend that. If Ellie talked about her super self, Hannah might not want to be friends anymore.

Hannah led the way into her bedroom. "Wait here," she told Ellie. "I'll try on my costume for you." She disappeared into the bathroom, and a few moments later, came twirling back out. "Ta-da!" she cheered, waving a feathery sword above her head. "I'm a pirate!"

Ellie's eyes widened at the costume. It was red and glittery, with black crisscrosses on the front. It made Hannah look like Peg Leg Pansy, swashbuckling super-villain of the high seas. She tried to think of something else to tell Hannah, but all that came out was: "You look great, not like a super-villain swashbuckler at all."

DANCE

Hannah's sword dropped. "Uh . . . okay," she replied. "Do you want to put on nail stickers? My mom bought ones with green-and-gold sparkles."

"Yeah!" Ellie agreed happily.

Hannah changed back into her normal, everyday clothes — the ones that didn't make her look like a super-villain. Then she found the stickers in her craft drawer. Together, the two girls decorated their nails and put matching sparkles on their pinkies. After Hannah's mom brought out fruit-and-cheese kabobs, they sat on ladybug beanbags and watched a video of Hannah's dance recital.

When the video ended, Ellie glanced at her watch. She had to get home! Time sure flew when she wasn't busy busting bad guys.

Hannah gave Ellie a tight hug. "Can you come back next weekend?" she asked. "You have to see the dance scrapbook I'm making. It's filled with pictures from all of my recitals. I've been working on it for so long, and I'm almost done. "

"I'll ask my mom," Ellie replied. She'd already promised to help pull weeds around the yard next weekend, but maybe she could use the Ultra Digger. Then she'd finish in no time!

Ellie waved goodbye and then headed home. The whole way back, she thought about how much fun she'd had with Hannah. They hadn't foiled a bank robbery or anything like that. But she'd still had a super time.

Ellie leaped inside her house and hopped into the kitchen. "Can I use the Ultra Digger in the yard?" she asked her parents. "I'll be careful with it this time. No more holes to China."

Mom and Dad were waiting for her at the table. From their stern faces, Ellie could tell they were more concerned about a different gadget.

"Ellie, where is the Ultra Remote?" Mom asked. "It's missing from my desk."

Ellie sighed. How could she keep a secret from her parents? They knew everything, being a couple of smarty-pants and all. "My powers were getting in the way at school," she confessed. "I took the remote to turn them off."

Her parents traded odd glances — the same ones they always seemed to be wearing when an invention wasn't working. "You turned off your super speed?" Dad asked.

"Uh-huh," Ellie replied.

"Your brainpower?"

"Uh-huh."

"And your X-ray vision?"

"Uh-huh," Ellie answered, "but not my muscle power. I need that to lift my backpack. That thing can get as heavy as an elephant android!"

Her parents stayed quiet, so Ellie kept talking. "I like having the remote," she explained. "It's helping me fit in better with the other kids. I'll put it back when I'm done. I promise."

Dad made a thinking face. Then he said, "I suppose that's fine. But use it carefully. The Ultra Remote is very powerful. It can stop anyone, even a superhero."

He's right about that! Ellie thought. And that was the whole point. "Thanks," she replied.

"Anything else going on at school?" Mom asked, softening. "Let me guess . . . is a mutant cheeseburger attacking the cafeteria? An evil chimp taking over the monkey bars? A super-villainous queen bee turning everybody into mindless drones?"

Ellie laughed. Her mom could say the silliest things. "Nope. Just the usual, ordinary stuff."

And that was how she liked third grade — ordinary, minus the extra.

CHAPTER 6

The Piece of Me Project

On Monday morning after math, Miss Little jingled her wind chime, which meant there was an important announcement. Ellie didn't need to read her teacher's mind to know that. Miss Little always used the chime for that reason.

Ellie closed her workbook. "You're doing better at estimating," she said to Dex. She had been helping him since Miss Little paired them up. Sure, Dex was a mastermind. But he was a mastermind at evil, not at rounding numbers.

Dex pushed up his nose like a pig. "Oink!" he snorted back. He looked like the super-villain Hogsbreath, only extra super villainous.

Ellie didn't let his piggy face bother her. She might have put her powers on hold. But she was still a superhero, and superheroes helped people — Hogsbreath face or no Hogsbreath face.

"I have wonderful news, third graders!" Miss Little exclaimed as the last chime sang. "We are starting a getting-to-know-you project. The project is called Piece of Me. For this assignment, you will share an item that is special to you. It should be something that makes you *you*."

"Can I share more than one item?" Owen asked. "I like collecting things. Right now I have a sock monkey collection, a dust bunny collection, a chip-clip collection, a . . ."

"Sharing one collection is just fine," Miss Little interrupted.

Amanda's hand waved wildly. "Can I bring my journal? That's where I keep my butterfly poems. I can even read one!"

"Your journal sounds lovely," Miss Little answered. "And any kind of collection, hobby, or craft would be great. Now, everyone, please take out a piece of paper and make a list of possible items. You will have today and tomorrow to choose one. Then on Thursday, we'll present our projects."

Papers flew and pencils scribbled as the class excitedly wrote down ideas.

"I'm bringing my model of the solar system," Joshua said. "I *love* making models. I've made one of a log cabin and Mount Rushmore. The solar system was the hardest. Making all those planets took for-EHHH-ver."

"I memorized the first poem from my journal," Amanda said. "It goes like this:

I have scales on my wings.
They are very beautiful things.
See me flying up so high.
I'm a butterfly in the sky."

The other kids at her table clapped, and Amanda brightened.

As everybody made his or her list, Ellie stared at the blank page in her notebook. She couldn't think of anything worth writing down. Ideas for extraordinary items floated around in her head. There was the red nose she'd pulled off the Clown Bandit. There was the newspaper article about how she'd caught Harry Knuckles, Winkopolis's baddest bad guy. Those items were okay for super Ellie. But if she shared that piece of herself, would she stop fitting in? Talking about her super self hadn't gone well on her first day. Everybody had acted like she'd had radioactive ants marching out of her ears.

All of a sudden, Ellie didn't feel so good. Her stomach churned like a giant tub of boiling hot sauce. She needed to leave. "Miss Little, may I go to the bathroom?" she asked.

Miss Little looked up from Owen's list and nodded. She'd been helping him decide which collection to share. Turned out, he had *a lot* of collections.

Ellie super speed-walked down the hallway to the bathroom. In the stall, she waited for her stomach to settle. She lost track of how long she stayed in there. But she knew she had to get back to class. If too much time went by, Miss Little would send a bathroom buddy after her.

As Ellie reached for the door, something poked her from inside her pocket. She pulled out the Ultra Remote. The remote! That would help her think of a regular item for her project. Quick as a click!

Ellie pressed the button. “Think.”

Her mind went blank. Then a picture of a meteor appeared.

“A meteor?” Ellie said, staring off into space. She *had* stopped a meteor from crashing into the moon. It was a big deal, and she was proud of saving the Moon People. But how could she share that item? It wasn’t exactly un-super.

Ellie clicked the remote again. “Think,” she said, a little louder this time.

In the meteor’s place, a fishing boat flashed.

Ellie rolled her eyes. Now the remote was reminding her of when she’d rescued the boat. It had sprung a leak, so she’d had to carry it back to shore.

MOST
HELPFUL

Ellie started to get annoyed. Why wasn't the remote working? She had to think of something *un*-extraordinary. "Think," she said, clicking the button over and over, "think, think . . . THINK!"

Click. She saw the baby hippo she had saved at the zoo. *Click.* She saw the soccer net she'd kicked the ball through. *Click.* She saw her *Most Helpful Citizen* ribbon from the mayor.

After one last click, a picture of the Ultra Remote appeared in Ellie's mind.

"Huh?" Ellie said. That didn't make any sense. With a frustrated sigh, she gave up and stuffed the remote away. Her parents had probably goofed when building it. Even geniuses made mistakes. That, along with asking questions, was how they got so smart.

Ellie trudged back to class. By the time she returned, all of her classmates had pages filled with ideas. Sinking into her seat, Ellie came face-to-face with one of the greatest challenges she'd ever faced — the Blank Page of Doom.

CHAPTER 7

Ellie's Brainstorm

The next day flew by faster than a runaway comet. Ellie had zero time to think of something un-superhero-ish for her project. Mainly because superhero-ish things kept getting in the way.

First, a flock of chicken-bots invaded the Ultras' kitchen. The evil Farmer Cyborg had sent them. He was after the Ultra Mind Scrambler, which could mix up somebody's thoughts. It also made super-fluffy scrambled eggs.

To get rid of the clucking crooks, Ellie found just the thing — the Ultra Noise Maker, set to BARKING DOG.

And on top of her superhero good deeds, there was homework.

Ugh, Ellie thought, looking up the term *totem pole* in her social studies textbook. *An ordinary super kid's work is never done.*

* * *

On Wednesday, Ellie opened her notebook during silent reading. She still needed to brainstorm a regular item for her Piece of Me project, and presentations were supposed to start tomorrow.

Ellie stared down at the Blank Page of Doom. She imagined herself filling it with ideas for a regular item. Eventually, her eyes crossed from staring so hard.

Finally, she wrote:

Blank Page of Doom: 1

Ellie: 0

Ellie laid down her pencil and picked up her head. All around the room, kids were reading quietly. Almost everyone had decided what to share. Miss Little had let those kids read while the rest of the class finished brainstorming.

Miss Little, who was wandering the rows to help, noticed Ellie's blank page. "Hmm," the teacher said, "it seems you're stuck. Would you like a hand?"

Ellie crossed her arms. "I can't think of an item for my project," she replied. "There's nothing I can share."

Miss Little thought for a moment. "Oh, I know! How about sharing your cape? The one you wore on your first day?"

My cape! Ellie thought. She perked up just thinking about it. Getting her cape had made her so happy.

"If I remember correctly, you said it helps you fly. It sounds like a super-special part of your life."

It is *a super-special part.* She shook her head. "No, that won't work."

Miss Little gave Ellie an encouraging wink. "Keep brainstorming. I'm sure you'll come up with something."

As her teacher walked away, Ellie looked around at her classmates who were reading. She really wanted to chill out and read *Ice Boy*. Dex had been hogging it all week long. Sure enough, when Ellie spotted him on the class comfy chair, he was flipping through the comic book. She frowned as he turned a page too hard and ripped off the corner.

At her desk, Hannah was looking at a ballet book. Her pirate costume would've been a perfect item for her project, but she'd told Ellie that she finished her dance scrapbook. She was excited about sharing that.

Ellie looked at the cover of Hannah's book. There was a picture of a ballerina in a sparkly tutu. Suddenly thunder rumbled inside Ellie's brain. She was having a brainstorm! *I know what I can share!*

Sweeping up her pencil, Ellie scratched out the score and scribbled down her idea. She showed Miss Little, who answered with a thumbs-up and a smile. Lightning flashed between Ellie's brain waves, making the classroom lights flicker.

"That's strange — I don't see any rain clouds," Miss Little said, looking out the window curiously. "How extraordinary."

* * *

After school, Ellie bounded into her parents' lab. She needed her mom's super know-it-all skills. "MOM!" she called. Her extraordinarily loud voice rattled an entire wall of thingamabobs.

Mrs. Ultra rounded the corner with an egg-shaped gadget. "Yikes!" she exclaimed. "I think the Moon People heard you. What's up?"

Just then, the gadget Mom was holding pumped out a puff of stinky smoke. Ellie pinched her nose. "Yuckola! What's that?"

"Sorry," Mom said. "It's our latest invention for B.R.A.I.N. — the Ultra Smell-O-Meter. It'll help fight villains like Professor Nose and the Sniffasaurus. It makes all sorts of odors, from the smell of shampoo to peeled onions. Right now, it's set to skunk."

Ellie made a face. No wonder it smelled like the time a skunk had sprayed Cyclops in the yard! "Do you know where my tutu is?" she asked.

"Are you interested in joining ballet again?" Mom asked. "You know, I just saw Madam Bernard at the grocery store. All she talked about was your recital performance. She was very impressed by your tornado . . . I mean, *pirouette*."

"No, no. It's for a project at school. We need to share something about ourselves. I'm going to talk about that."

"It's in your closet," Mom answered. "You'll also find a special surprise in there from Dad and me. Since school has been tough, we wanted to give you something that'll cheer you up."

"Thanks!" Ellie rushed out the doorway. She would've hugged her mom, but it was too risky. She didn't want to end up getting Skunk-O-Metered.

Ellie flew into her room and flung her closet open. Folded neatly on the shelf was her cape. It looked exactly the same as when she'd first seen it. Except this time, her name had been stitched across the back.

"A real superhero cape!" Ellie exclaimed.

Ellie whisked the cape down and around her shoulders. Standing tall, she admired herself in the mirror. She looked like an honest-to-goodness

ELLIE
ULTRA

superhero. And now she had an honest-to-goodness super name to match.

While striking her best hero pose, Ellie saw something sparkle in the closet. It was her tutu! She took off her cape and grabbed the frilly pouf.

Pushing her comic books to the floor, Ellie flopped down on her bed. She looked at the tutu for a long time. It was pretty — and pretty regular. But the idea of choosing that for her presentation seemed wrong.

Ellie finally had the missing piece of her Piece of Me project. So why did it feel like a piece of her was *still* missing?

CHAPTER 8

Bouncy Balls to the Rescue

Before Ellie knew it, presentation day had arrived. After gym class, she went to her locker. She grabbed her tutu and mentally rehearsed the normal things she was going to say about it.

The classroom was bustling when she returned. Everybody was hopping around, showing off what they'd brought. Amanda was reciting a butterfly poem from her journal. Joshua was standing beside his solar system model. Taped to the sun was a sign that read: *DO NOT TOUCH*.

A crowd had gathered around Hannah, who was proudly holding up her dance scrapbook. It was covered in stickers of tap shoes and ballet slippers. In fancy glitter-glue letters, the words *My Dance Life* were scrolled across the front. With all the decorations, it looked really special.

Hannah beamed as she opened to the first page. "Here's me at my first recital," she said, pointing to a picture of her wearing a teacup on her head. "I danced to 'I'm a Little Teapot.' It was so fun!"

Suddenly a purple bouncy ball came flying out of nowhere. It bounced off the scrapbook and into Ellie's hand.

"Stop that ball!" Owen hollered, pushing through everybody. Under his arm, he held a shoe box that rattled with his bouncy ball collection.

Ellie handed over the ball, and Owen's cheeks got pink. He scooped it back into the box and closed the lid.

"Settle down, class!" Miss Little rang her wind chime. "I know you're excited to share your Piece of Me projects. Please take your seats, and let's begin."

As the kids scattered to their desks, Ellie trailed behind. She kept thinking about how happy Hannah was to share her scrapbook. Ellie sure didn't feel the same way about her tutu.

Ellie stuffed the tutu under her chair. *If only I could've shared my cape,* she thought. *Too late now.*

Payton volunteered to go first. She held up a woven picture of a big blue whale and talked about her picture-weaving hobby. The whale was made out of the rest of her mom's yarn.

Next Owen showed off his bouncy ball collection. He had many kinds of bouncy balls: glow-in-the-dark ones, ones with different faces, and some with swirly colors.

"How many balls are in your collection?" Miss Little asked.

"Thirty-seven," Owen replied. "But my dad said I couldn't bring them all."

When Owen finished his presentation, he took a bow. His shoe box tilted forward, and a spiky ball rolled out. Miss Little caught up to it under Ellie's chair.

Miss Little noticed the tutu. "What a beautiful skirt, Ellie. Why don't you share your item next?"

Ellie managed a smile, even though she felt like her excitement had been gobbled by hungry piranhas. "I guess," she replied. She picked herself up and wiggled into the poufy circle. The elastic waistband squeezed tighter than Octobaby, super-villain of doo-doo and destruction.

MATH
QUIZ
$2x^2+5x+2$
$x+2)(x+1)$

"I was in ballet, and this is my tutu," Ellie began. "I learned lots of things, like how to a *plié*" — she bent her knees — "and *relevé*" — she went up onto her toes. "I did those moves during my recital." She talked some more about her routine, remembering not to mention her super move, the Tornado Twirl.

The kids clapped when Ellie finished. The sound tickled her ears, making her smile. She didn't feel so bad anymore about not sharing her cape. Just like the superheroes in her comic books, Ellie had successfully hidden her super self. She . . . belonged.

"Wait!" Hannah shouted. "Ellie, do a *pirouette*! You do the best ones!"

"Yeah! Do a *pirouette*!" Amanda and Payton chimed in.

Everybody watched Ellie, waiting for her to perform. But the only thing turning was her face, which was now as red as a chocolate-cake-flavored beet! She needed the Ultra Remote to control her super speed. Too bad it was inside her desk. Without it, she would twist into a tornado!

Just then, Owen let out a squeak. "Uh-oh!"

The class whipped around to see Owen's shoe box hit the floor. The lip flipped off, sending balls bouncing in every direction.

Miss Little's forehead fell into her hand. "Please sit down, Ellie," she said as a smiley-face ball bounced past her. "We'll hear the next presentation in a moment. First, let's help Owen clean up."

While the other kids collected Owen's collection, Ellie yanked off her tutu. She took a deep sigh of relief. A bunch of bouncy balls had rescued her from becoming extraordinary Ellie. Of course, her super self could have gathered all the balls in no time. But her powers belonged inside. Ellie was sure of it — well . . . maybe not *super* sure.

CHAPTER 9

Ellie Ultra

After Payton had rounded up the last bouncy ball, Miss Little put the lid on Owen's collection. His shoe box was now sitting quietly next to Dex's shareable item, a remote-controlled Action Smash Truck, on the teacher's desk. All through morning announcements, Dex had smashed the truck into Ellie's chair. Ellie had been close to melting it into a plastic lump, but Miss Little had gotten her hands on it first.

When everyone else had finished presenting, Miss Little gave the truck back to Dex. "It's your turn to present," she said. "You can show us how your item works. Just remember to be careful around the art caddy and storage baskets — and the flowerpot."

Dex smiled wickedly, rubbing his hands together like the evil mastermind he was. Obviously, he was plotting something. Whatever it was, Ellie knew it meant trouble.

On the floor, Dex built an obstacle course. He stacked books and arranged crayon cups. Then he set down his four-wheeled fiend. "I know everything about Action Smash Trucks," he said. "This one is called Goliath, and it can knock down anything. If you don't believe me, watch."

The class leaned forward as Dex pulled a remote control out of his hoodie. Ellie edged closer to get a better look too.

Oddly enough, Dex's remote looked just like the Ultra Remote. The only difference between the two was the Action Smash stamp on the back of Dex's.

With a click, Goliath's headlights flashed on. With two clicks, it lurched forward. Down went the books. Down went the cups. Dex stood over his minion's mess, grinning approvingly.

As Goliath trampled some crayons, Ellie turned away from the motorized mayhem. Her super ears had caught wind of a familiar noise outside. It whirred like a fan, coming closer and closer and . . .

CRASH! Out of nowhere, a spaceship crashed into the room. It circled slowly above the class, its lights flashing this way and that.

It was Captain Blob and the Goo Crew!

Ellie blinked as the saucer floated overhead. Was her super sight playing a trick on her? Last week, the aliens had tried to drop in on her house. *That* she could believe. If they wanted to control the universe like her mom had said, they'd need an Ultra invention. But why would they come to school?

She gasped. The Ultra Remote! Opening her desk, she quickly grabbed the remote and hid it in her sock.

The spaceship settled onto the United States of America rug, taking up all fifty states, including Alaska. The top flipped off, and a group of blobs wiggled out. Each one stood no taller than the average third grader and had a body that jiggled like a mound of jelly.

"I amppptth Captain Blob," announced the jiggliest of them all, his tongue spitting green goo. "My crew and I have comepptth for the Ultra Remote. With it, we will take over the planet. Then . . . THE UNIVERSE!"

Miss Little shrieked. Payton and Owen's mouths hung open. Hannah hugged her dance scrapbook. Dex stared blankly as Captain Blob oozed forward.

GOLIATH

The captain swiped Dex's remote away. "At last, the Ultra Remote is ours!" he said triumphantly.

Captain Blob raised the remote like it was a trophy for World's Worst Super-Villain.

Ellie shook her head. Super-villains were like that, always celebrating for a no-good reason. *If I'm lucky, Captain Blob will think Dex's remote is the real thing,* she thought. *Then he'll take his goopy friends and go.*

Unfortunately, luck was not on Ellie's side.

Turning over the remote, Captain Blob eyeballed it suspiciously. "Hmmpptth?" he said, spotting the words *ACTION SMASH*. "This isn't an Ultra invention! The real remote must be hiding somewhere." He flung a pointed finger at his crew. "Find it!"

The other blobs gave a slimy salute and then split up to search the classroom. One blob yanked the yarn out of Payton's picture. Another one left green smudges all over Amanda's journal.

"Give that back!" Joshua shouted as a blob picked apart his solar system model. "Do you know how long that took to make?"

Ellie watched in horror. The blobs weren't just hunting for the remote. They were messing up everybody's projects! How could she stop them? Using her powers would make her stick out again. The only other solution she could think of was handing over her parents' gadget.

Maybe an intergalactic takeover wouldn't be that bad, Ellie thought. *There might not be any more homework . . .*

"No!" Hannah cried.

Ellie turned around just as a blob snatched Hannah's scrapbook. The blob peeled off a picture of Hannah, who was dressed like a tap-dancing ice cream cone. It opened wide, then swallowed the picture whole.

Hannah needed help. So did the rest of Ellie's friends. How could she sit there and do nothing? That would be really un-super of her.

Across the room, Dex and Captain Blob were going head-to-head in a tug-of-war over Goliath. "That's my truck!" Dex shouted, trying to pull it away.

With Dex keeping the captain busy, Ellie decided to make her move. She blinked and turned herself invisible. Then she snuck past the blobs, heading for the window.

As she passed Captain Blob, her curls accidentally tickled his nose.

"Ah . . . ah . . . ," the captain sniffled.

He was going to sneeze! Ellie ducked out of the way.

"Ah-CHOOMPPTTH!" Captain Blob let loose a shower of blob boogers.

Dex let go of his truck. “GROSS!” he yelled. His hands were dripping with green goo.

Ellie felt bad for Dex, but she couldn’t worry about him getting slimed. She had a much slimier super-villain to worry about. How could she get rid of Captain Blob? She needed a super idea from something that was equally super — her comic books!

CHAPTER 10

Blob Ballet

Soaring through the air, Ellie zoomed over rooftops. She punched the sky with her fist, leaving behind a trail of donut-hole clouds. To anybody on the ground, Ellie looked like a blazing fireball. But on the inside, she felt like a blown-out birthday candle. Her friends' stuff was being destroyed, all because she'd brought the Ultra Remote to school. She had to make things right.

Seconds later, Ellie burst into her house and whooshed upstairs. Her parents were on the other side of town at B.R.A.I.N. headquarters, so she was home alone.

Rummaging through her comic books, Ellie tried to find a way to battle the alien blobs. She scanned the first five issues of the *Zombie-Eating Pumpkin,* then moved on to *Mind Surfer vs. Dr. Wipe Out.* Nothing! Her comics had great ideas for squashing bloodsucking bananas and scaring off prehistoric squirrels from Planet Nut. But how could Ellie fight space goop? If only another superhero could help.

"How about you, Super Fluffy?" Ellie asked her stuffed dog. "Could you help me stop those slimeballs?" Under his floppy ears, Super Fluffy sat quietly. Ellie sighed. Even if he were real, Super Fluffy would probably prefer chasing cats to stopping super-villains.

Just then — *POW!* — a super thought struck. "Super-villain cats!" Ellie hollered. "Of course!" She dug into the pile and found *Maximum Mouse #2: Attack of the Trash Monster.*

In the comic book, Maximum Mouse was protecting all that was good and cheesy in Cheesetown. Suddenly Kitty Litter pounced. Kitty was Maximum's archenemy, and he was always trying to spoil everything. This time he'd set a garbage monster loose!

Kitty's monster went to work trashing Cheesetown. It dropped juice boxes and tossed out toilet paper rolls until Maximum scampered into action. The super squeaker raced around the stinky creation, picking off things like sandwich bags, old sneakers, and crushed soup cans. Maximum plucked away every piece of trash until there was nothing left of the monster. Kitty was hissing mad!

Ellie thought about Captain Blob. From head to toe, he was a heaping helping of goo. Could he come apart like Kitty Litter's monster? She took out the remote. "Guess I'll find out!"

As she left, Ellie made a quick stop at her closet. Then, with a flash of pink, she took off into the air, flying much faster than before.

* * *

Back in the classroom, the blobs were still searching for the Ultra Remote. They had turned everybody's project upside-down and inside out. Their mess was out-of-this-world, even for aliens.

Joshua's planets were plucked from their orbit, and Mars was missing.

"My collection!" Owen yelled as a blob drooled over the bouncy balls.

The blob smacked its lips. "Mmmpptth . . . bubble gumpptth!"

Ellie swooped into the doorway. "Stop!" she ordered, hands on her hips. Her cape waved powerfully under the blowing air conditioner.

The blobs took one look at her and stopped in their slippery tracks. For a four-foot-tall superhero, Ellie was very intimidating.

Captain Blob needed more convincing than his minions. Across his face, an evil grin spread like butter on toast. "Who are *you*?" he said with a snort.

Ellie felt her knees go wobbly. She could tell the super-villain didn't take her seriously. If she was going to stand up against him, she couldn't be afraid to show her super self.

"I'm Ellie Ultra," Ellie bravely announced. She held up the Ultra Remote. If Captain Blob saw she had it, maybe he'd leave her friends' stuff alone. "I have the remote, but I'm not letting you take it."

Captain Blob frowned. A thwarted plan could always turn a super-villain into a grouch potato. "Is that so? Well then . . ." He quickly dropped Dex's truck and lifted Dex off the ground by the hood. "I'll take this boy instead. I've always wanted a pet human."

"Hey, let go!" Dex yelled.

Ellie watched as Dex dangled like a rotting apple. He was mean to her, but she couldn't let him get turned into a space pet. That would be wrong. Besides, she didn't want to get a stop sign on her behavior chart.

Kicking up her speedy heels, she ran to her chair and scooped up her tutu, which was still sitting where she'd left it. Then she leaped over the captain and — *SQUISH!* — pulled the sparkly skirt down over his head. Dex immediately slipped out of the villain's grip.

"I-I-I c-c-can't move!" Captain Blob sputtered, wobbling from side to side. The tutu held him as tightly as Octobaby clutching his blanky.

Ellie aimed the Ultra Remote at him. It was time for some ballet dancing, alien blob-style. *"Plié!"* she commanded with a click.

Captain Blob looked surprised as he sank into a graceful squat. He could only obey, now completely under the remote's control. "Release me this instant!" he blubbered.

Ellie clicked the remote again. *"Relevé!"* From his squat, the captain rose up onto his tiptoes.

"Spin!" Ellie ordered with another click. Captain Blob pirouetted once around. He twirled so quickly that slime flew off him.

Ellie grinned. Her idea was working! "Spin!" she repeated. Captain Blob whipped around and around, spraying more slime as he spun.

Ellie kept clicking. "Spin, spin, spin!" she cried.

The captain turned and turned. With every twirl, more and more slime sprayed. Before Ellie's eyes, Captain Blob was shrinking! After one final *pirouette,* he disappeared. Ellie's tutu fell with a *sploosh!* into the green puddle below.

The other blobs murmured angrily. It was hard to figure out what they were saying. But from their snorts and snarls, Ellie knew it wasn't good.

"Attack!" they growled, charging across the room.

Ellie scanned the room and spotted a tangled mess of yarn — the remains of the whale picture — in Payton's lap. She swept up one end and raced in circles around the blobs, tying them into a slimy spool. Then she tossed them into their spaceship, flipped the top closed, and gave the spaceship a super-strong kick.

BLAM! The blobs went spinning out of the window. They tore through the atmosphere, never to return again.

"Score!" Ellie cheered. She pointed to the sky and did a victory dance. She had defeated the blobs, saving her friends, her teacher, and the world — maybe even the universe! This called for a celebration!

But when she glanced around, Ellie realized she was the only one celebrating. Miss Little and the other kids just stared at her, totally shocked. The Piece of Me projects — now in *actual* pieces — were scattered from one corner to another.

Dex scowled at Ellie. "Super Blooper strikes again," he muttered, going back to wiping boogers off his truck.

Ellie's excitement melted away as fast as Ice Boy on a hot day. Being super had helped her save the day, but it had also made her stick out like never before.

Before anyone else could say a word, Ellie hurried out of the classroom. She was sure she'd lost her friends. Why should she stick around to hear what they thought of her now? She dragged her cape the whole way home, feeling lonelier than ever.

CHAPTER 11

Doomed?

The next morning, Mom popped into Ellie's room. "Time for school, superhero!"

Ellie pulled her blanket over her head. She didn't want to face anybody, not after making a super blooper of herself the day before. "Can I stay home?" she croaked. "I can clean up the finger paints in Cyclops's tank. He wants to start a new hobby . . . knitting."

Mom peeked at Ellie under the blanket. "I know you're worried about yesterday, but give your friends some credit. They like you, super skills and all. Besides, you belong in school. What if a mutant cheeseburger attacks the cafeteria?"

Ellie cracked a smile. Her mom knew just how to lift her spirits.

"Oh! That reminds me," Mom added. "Your tutu is all clean. I'm glad Dad and I got the Ultra Washing Machine working again. Blob gunk is hard to get out!"

* * *

When Ellie arrived at school, Mr. Cleveland was waiting at the main entrance. He greeted her with a serious face instead of his usual smile. "Ellie, I need to speak with you in my office," he said firmly.

Ellie's stomach dropped as she followed him inside. Going to the principal's office was like stepping into a super-villain's lair. She doubted Mr. Cleveland had any giant hairy spiders hanging around, but it still made her worry.

"Do you know why you're here, Ellie?" Mr. Cleveland asked as he sat down behind his desk.

Ellie shook her head. She'd been too nervous to read his mind and find out.

"I heard what happened in Miss Little's classroom," Mr. Cleveland began. "Blobs have never visited Winkopolis Elementary School, and I hope they don't again. Their visit was extraordinary. It surprised your teacher and classmates, but they were more surprised by your behavior. I heard it was also quite extraordinary."

Ellie's worries doubled. The blobs *were* extraordinary, and Mr. Cleveland didn't think they belonged in school — which was true. Did he also feel that way about third-grade superheroes?

Mr. Cleveland continued: "Because of your extraordinary behavior, I need to give you this . . ." He reached into a folder and pulled out a piece of paper with a bunch of words on it.

Ellie scooted to the edge of her seat and scanned the certificate. It read:

Winkopolis Elementary School's
HERO STUDENT AWARD

This certificate is awarded to: Ellie Ultra

For: Saving your class from a super-villain invasion

Signed: Mr. Cleveland, principal

Ellie couldn't believe it. She was getting an award for being a superhero! Her eyes lit up as she read the certificate over and over.

"Every school needs a hero," Mr. Cleveland said with a smile, "and we're happy to have one who's as super as you. Now, if you'll follow me, your class has something to say to you too."

Ellie stood up and followed Mr. Cleveland down the hallway. She beamed at her award the whole time. As she stepped inside the classroom, applause filled the air. Miss Little and the kids crowded around, cheering, "YAAAY for Ellie! YAY!"

Ellie was stunned. "You're happy to see me?" she asked. "But aren't you mad about your projects? The blobs ruined your things, and it was all because they were looking for what I had. I messed up everything."

"I can always make another picture," Payton said, patting Ellie's shoulder. "My mom found more yarn."

"And besides," Owen added, "those blobs wanted to take over the world. If you hadn't stopped them, they would've turned us all into space pets — not just Dex."

Everybody looked at Dex. At his desk, he was making his rottenest face yet.

Ellie rolled her eyes. The least he could do was be nice to her. After all, she'd rescued him! But when did a super-villain ever thank a superhero? Never, the last time she'd checked.

Hannah wrapped her arms around Ellie. "You're not just a superhero — you're a super friend!" Hannah said. "A *real* super friend!"

Ellie's heart leaped higher than a kangaroo on a jet-powered pogo stick. She felt super. Actually, she felt more than super. She was their friend, and *that* felt extraordinary.

That day, everyone got used to having extraordinary Ellie around. During math, the class learned how to round numbers to the nearest quadrillion. When they ran relay races in gym, Ellie helped her team win — again and again.

That afternoon, when Joshua couldn't find Mars from his solar system model, Ellie scanned the

classroom. Her X-ray vision solved the mystery of the missing planet. Mars was in the Mystery Box!

"Have a super weekend!" Miss Little told her students at the end of the day.

"I hope it's not too super," Ellie said. "Farmer Cyborg's chicken-bots keep showing up, and they're getting mechanical feathers all over the place!"

Miss Little looked like Ellie had laid a chicken-bot egg. Then she replied, "I bet those villains are no match for Ellie Ultra."

Ellie smiled. *For an ordinary teacher, Miss Little is pretty super,* she thought.

* * *

When she got home, Ellie flew like a whirlwind into her parents' lab. At their worktable, Mom and Dad were drawing up plans for a new invention. The rush of air sent their drawings flying.

AWARD

"Look at what I got!" Ellie shouted. She held out the certificate as papers rained down.

"Good work, Super Student!" Dad said.

Ellie dug the Ultra Remote out of her backpack. "Turns out, you were right. I don't need the remote," she said. "The kids like having a superhero around!"

Mom put her arm around Ellie. "They like you because you're a super kid, powers or no powers."

"That award would look great in your room," Dad added. "Right next to your *Most Helpful Citizen* ribbon."

"Super-genius idea!" Ellie exclaimed. She raced upstairs and plucked a pushpin from her bulletin board. After pinning up the certificate, she stepped back to admire it. It had been extraordinary to share her super self, but the truth was, her friends didn't seem to care about her powers one way or the other. They liked Ellie for Ellie. And that was the most extraordinary thing of all.

GLOSSARY

admire (ad-MIRE) — to like and respect someone

altitude (AL-ti-tood) — the height of something above the ground

archenemy (AHRCH-EN-uh-mee) — someone's main enemy

blooper (BLOO-per) — an embarrassing mistake made in public

extraordinary (ek-STROR-duh-ner-ee) — very unusual or remarkable

meteor (MEE-tee-ur) — a piece of rock or metal from space that enters Earth's atmosphere at high speed, burns, and forms streaks of light as it falls to Earth

mutant (MYOOT-uhnt) — a living thing that has developed different characteristics because of a change in its parents' genes

pirouette (pir-oo-ET) — a ballet move that consists of a full turn on the front of one foot

punctual (PUHNGK-choo-uhl) — on time

radioactive (ray-dee-oh-AK-tiv) — if something is radioactive, it is made up of atoms whose nuclei have broken down, giving off harmful radiation

recital (ri-SYE-tuhl) — a musical performance by a single performer or by a small group of musicians or dancers

venomous (VEN-uh-muhs) — poisonous

villain (VIL-uhn) — a wicked person, often an evil character in a play

TALK ABOUT ELLIE!

1. Ellie's superhero cape is super special to her — she had to wait months to get it! Talk about an object that is special to you. What makes it so important?

2. Ellie has lots of different superpowers, including X-ray vision, super speed, and flying. Imagine you are a superhero. What superpower would you want to have? Talk about your choice and explain why you picked it.

3. Do you think it was right of Ellie to take the Ultra Remote without her parents' permission? Talk about some other ways she could have handled the situation.

EXPRESS YOURSELF!

1. Ellie is worried that she won't fit in at her new school because her superpowers make her different, but our differences are what make us unique! Write a paragraph about what makes you special and unique.

2. Starting at a new school can be tough, even without superpowers. Have you ever been the new kid? Write a paragraph about how you felt. If you haven't, write a paragraph imagining how you would feel and how you would deal with the situation.

3. At the end of this story, the principal gives Ellie a certificate celebrating her actions. Use your imagination and create your own Hero Student Award. You can either give it to a friend or keep it for yourself.

ABOUT THE AUTHOR

Gina Bellisario is an ordinary grown-up who can do many extraordinary things. She can make things disappear, such as a cheeseburger or a grass stain. She can create a masterpiece out of glitter glue and shoelaces. She can even thwart a messy room with her super cleaning power! Gina lives in Park Ridge, Illinois, not too far from Winkopolis, with her husband and their super kids.

ABOUT THE ILLUSTRATOR

Jessika von Innerebner loves creating — especially when it inspires and empowers others to make the world a better place. She landed her first illustration job at the age of seventeen and hasn't looked back since. Jess is an illustrator who loves humor and heart and has colored her way through projects with Disney.com, Nickelodeon, Fisher-Price, and Atomic Cartoons, to name a few. In her spare moments, Jess can be found long-boarding, yoga-ing, dancing, adventuring to distant lands, and laughing with friends. She currently lives in sunny Kelowna, Canada.

READ THE REST OF ELLIE ULTRA'S EXTRAORDINARY ADVENTURES!